CARL'S SUMMER VACATION

Carl's Summer Vacation

Alexandra Day

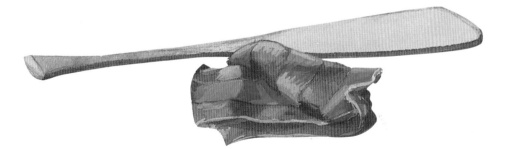

FARRAR STRAUS GIROUX

NEW YORK

Many thanks to Rory Cacilie Eggler and her family, Christina Darling, Rabindranath Darling, the Anderson family (especially Alex), the Krauters, Christine Alar, and Lafcadio Darling for their cooperation

Distributed in Canada by Douglas & McIntyre Ltd.

Color separations by Chroma Graphics PTE Ltd.

Printed and bound in China by South China Printing Co. Ltd.

Designed by Irene Metaxatos

First edition, 2008

1 3 5 7 9 10 8 6 4 2

www.fsgkidsbooks.com

Library of Congress Control Number: 2006935668

ISBN-13: 978-0-374-31085-1
ISBN-10: 0-374-31085-8

The Carl character originally appeared in Good Dog, Carl *by Alexandra Day, published by Green Tiger Press.*

"We sure have a lot to do this afternoon to get the cabin cleaned up and dinner ready. The Harrises are coming, you know."

"You two have a good nap so you'll be ready to go see the fireworks tonight."

"You're out!"

"No, I'm not. The dog's not
on your team."

"It's fan interference."

"He's not a fan. He's a dog!"

"Oh, look! The boat races are starting."

"It's getting late. We better think about going."

"Carl! Madeleine! Time to wake up.
Dinner's almost ready."

"I don't know what's wrong with these two.
They didn't eat, and they're exhausted even
though they had a long nap."